First published in Great Britain 2020 by Farshore
This edition published 2023 by Dean, part of Farshore
An imprint of HarperCollins*Publishers*
1 London Bridge Street, London SE1 9GF
www.farshore.co.uk

HarperCollins*Publishers*
Macken House, 39/40 Mayor Street Upper,
Dublin 1, D01 C9W8, Ireland

Text copyright © Adam and Charlotte Guillain 2020
Illustrations copyright © Sam Lloyd 2020
The authors and illustrator have asserted their moral rights.

ISBN 978 0 0086 1719 6
Printed in China
001

A CIP catalogue record for this title is available from the British Library.

MIX
Paper | Supporting
responsible forestry
FSC™ C007454

This book is produced from independently certified FSC™ paper
to ensure responsible forest management.

For more information visit: www.harpercollins.co.uk/green

ONE BANANA, TWO BANANAS

ADAM AND CHARLOTTE GUILLAIN

ILLUSTRATED BY SAM LLOYD

DEAN

three bananas, **four,**

snoozing in the garden when . . .

DING-DONG!

Who's at the door?

Welcome to Banana Bungalow

Five bananas, **six** bananas, **seven** bananas . . .

Eight

bananas in pyjamas
bouncing on the beds.

"Upsydaisy!"

shout bananas, standing on their heads.

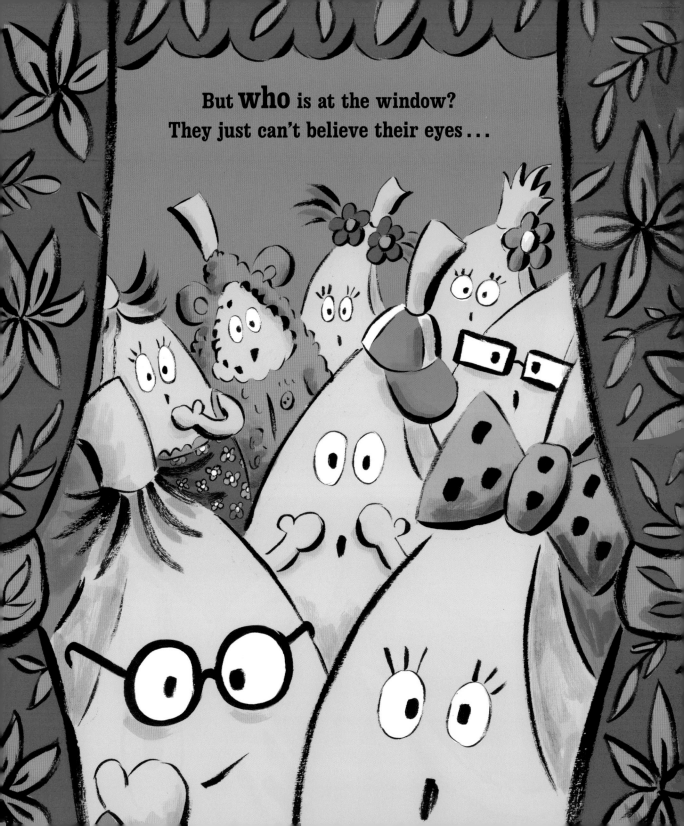

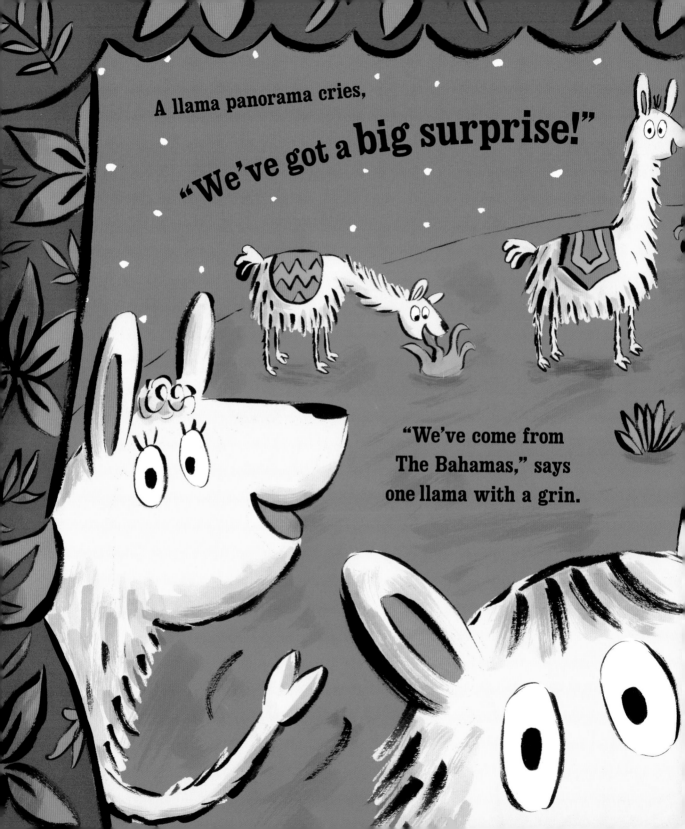

A llama panorama cries,

"We've got a **big surprise!**"

"We've come from
The Bahamas," says
one llama with a grin.

"We're going to have a llama race – you're welcome to join in."

Eight bananas leap off llamas –

Monkey licks his lips.

"Yikes!
What's that?" cries Monkey
as he stumbles and he slips!

A pair of super new bananas
come to make up **ten.**

Ten bananas shout at Monkey,

"**Don't** chase us **again!**"

But Monkey's feeling hungry and he doesn't care at all.
He scares the poor bananas as he leaps and makes them...

Ten bananas in pyjamas, swimming for their lives,
Chased by ten piranhas baring teeth as sharp as knives.

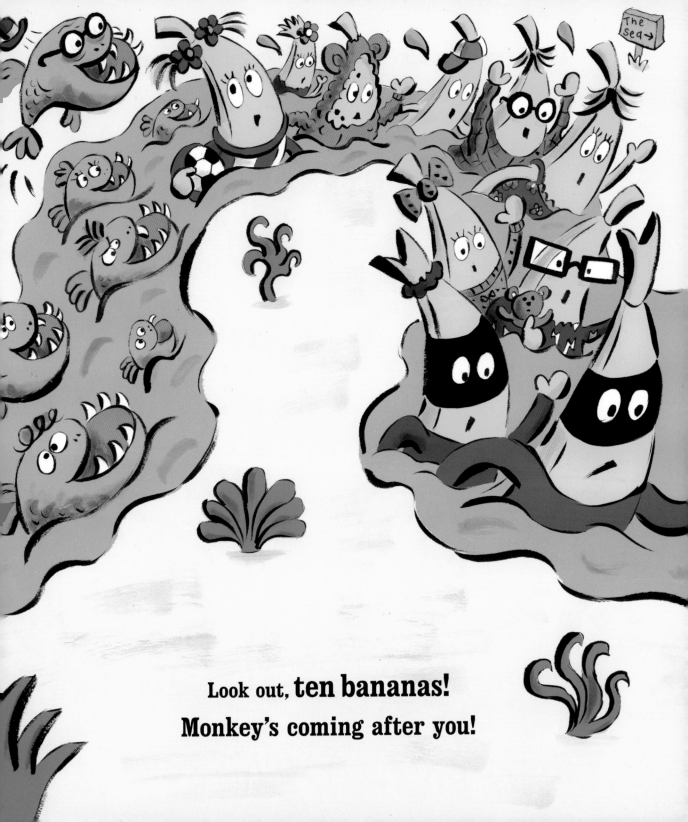

Look out, **ten bananas!**
Monkey's coming after you!

Ten bananas panic – how much longer can they float?

But look – across the water speeds...

. . . a fast banana boat!

"We're sorry!" ten bananas cheer,
"We **will** not be your **lunch!**"

And **you** can never catch us
as we're such
a clever bunch!"